Welcome!

Dear Reader,

Welcome to a world of imagination!

My First Story was designed for 5-7 year-olds as an introduction to creative writing and to promote an enjoyment of reading and writing from an early age.

The simple, fun storyboards give even the youngest and most reluctant writers the chance to become interested in literacy by giving them a framework within which to shape their ideas. Pupils could also choose to write without the storyboards, allowing older children to let their creativity flow as much as possible, encouraging the use of imagination and descriptive language.

We believe that seeing their work in print will inspire a love of reading and writing and give these young writers the confidence to develop their skills in the future.

There is nothing like the imagination of children, and this is reflected in the creativity and individuality of the stories in this anthology. I hope you'll enjoy reading their first stories as much as we have.

Jenni Harrison
Editorial Manager

Ima ine...

Each child was given the beginning of a story and then chose one of five storyboards, using the pictures and their imagination to complete the tale. You can view the storyboards at the end of this book.

There was also the option to create their own story using a blank template.

The Beginning...

One sunny day, Emma and Ben were walking the dog.

Suddenly, the dog started barking at a magic door hidden in a tree.

They opened the door and it took them to...

... what is on the other side of the door? Tell us your story!

ADVENTURES FROM THE UK
CONTENTS

Winner:

Tabitha Selby-Boothroyd (7) -   1
Danson Primary School, Welling

**Belvedere Infant School,
Belvedere**

Lyla-Grace Ruby Mehmet (7)	2
Talha Amzad (7)	4
Lucas Suter (6)	5
Layla Ong (6)	6
Zachary Derry (6)	7
Barnabas Bakos (7)	8
Jasleen Sandhu (7)	9
Vinnie-Joe Fagan (7)	10
Lucas Suter (6)	11
Annastasi Zan-Bi-Nation (6)	12
Cody Wiecek (6)	13
Honey-Rae Williams (6)	14
Tommy Nicholls Aird (7)	15
Alice Elizabeth Brooks (7)	16
Aniq Olorunteleola Okin (5)	17
Pavandeep Singh Dhesi (6)	18
Emanuela Ciobanu (6)	19
Jemima Oyeneye (7)	20
Nifemi Ayorinde-Salami (7)	21
Joshua Ayibatin (8)	22
Lola Stroud (7)	23
Jessica Kainth (6)	24
Layla Allia Bestford (6)	25
Dixie Ellis Wainwright (6)	26
Zahra Gerasimova (6)	27
Ryan Xuereb (6)	28
Lucas Shane Hawkins (8)	29
Kayden Eve (6)	30
Ethan Williams-Smith (7)	31
Ty'ree Zan-Bi-Nation (6)	32

Joseph Emmanuel (7)	33
Khushi Bajwa (7)	34
Lilie El Kedhri (5)	35
Maximus Scott (6)	36
Aimee Charlotte Garrard-Dinnadge (6)	37
Amber Grace Micetich (6) & Henry	38
Prabhbir Singh Atwal (6)	39
Georgie Lynn Hanscombe (7)	40
Logan Collis (6)	41

Danson Primary School, Welling

Layla Doris Ward (6)	42
Sophia McAvoy (7)	44
Charlotte Galbraith (7)	45
Mai Poppy Greenhead (7)	46
Aarush Devalpalli (6)	47
Finley Penney (6)	48
Balpreet Kaur Sangar (6)	49
Michael Inioluwa Hassan (7)	50
Luca Blake (6)	51
Penelope Hynes (6)	52
Lucy Horne (6)	53
Brooke Perring (6)	54
Cali Cato (7)	55
Archie Mark Berry (5)	56
Ryan Poudel (6)	57

Drapers Mills Primary Academy, Margate

Daisy Deal (6)	58
Tiffany Shannon (6)	59
Danielius Juscuis (6)	60
Ethan Rattray (6)	61

Finberry Primary School, Ashford

Ewan Murphy (6)	62
Rose Eliana Finn (5)	63
Jessica Davis (5)	64
Lawk Abdulkareem (6)	65
Tyler Gardiner	66
Nshira Yaw Preko (6)	67

Horizon Primary Academy, Swanley

Lilly Davies (6)	68
Tasanee Lamai Purser (6)	69
Deborah Teniola Adeyemi (6)	70
Lily Bassett (6)	71
Katherine Sophie Faith Jefferys (6)	72
Prince Hopkins (6)	73
Kieran Duffey (5)	74
Ella Stephens (5)	75
Brandon Lampard (6)	76
George Benjamin Hughes (6)	77

Lawley Primary School, Lawley

Sienna Jaina Dhiraj (6)	78
Tegan Walters (6)	79
Emily Harrison (6)	80
Isla Grace Edwards (6)	81
Daisy Godfrey (6)	82
Megan Broadhead (6)	83
Lucy Olivia Mantle (6)	84
Sam Wright (6)	85
Katie Snik (6)	86
Lily-Dee Smith (6)	87
Archie Charman (7)	88
Pennie Rose Whitehouse (6)	89
Mia Jenks (5)	90
Lexie Hendrie (6)	91
Noah Dungey (6)	92
Jake Sheen (5)	93
Sebastien Troy Smith (6)	94
Niall Corrigan (6)	95
Oscar Chamera (6)	96

Isaac Oliver Darbyshire (5)	97
Jack Oliver Jones (6)	98
Angel Antwi (5)	99
Lyra Jones (5)	100
Ray Joseph Malone (6)	101
Elle Clifton (6)	102
Grace Simpson (6)	103
Emma Alice Wagg (5)	104
Darcy Glaze (6)	105
Joshua Williams (6)	106
Daisy Iris Dawes (6)	107
Euan O'Neil (6)	108
Jack Robert Hughes (5)	109
Lilia Green (6)	110
Peramvir Chaudhari (6)	111
Jacoby Perry (6)	112
Charlotte Williams (6)	113
Manahal Maqbool (6)	114
Logan Round (6)	115
Maddie French (6)	116
Ava McGlynn (6)	117
Lexi Watson (5)	118
Erin Rogers (5)	119
Mikael Hasnain (6)	120
William Augustus Bear Jones (5)	121
Millie Bracken (6)	122
Lilliana Jean Corsentino (6)	123
Eva Kaur Sandhu (6)	124

Wymondley JMI School, Little Wymondley

Poppy Ann Hannah (6)	125
Heer Trushar Thakkar (5)	126
Alice Philippa Bestford (6)	128
Jessica Stappard (5)	130
Daisy Elizabeth Fraser (7)	131
Freddie Moore (6)	132
Isaac Page (6)	133
William Watts (6)	134
Alfie Robin Handley (8)	135

The Stories

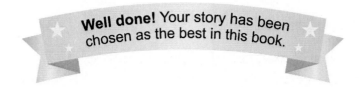

Well done! Your story has been chosen as the best in this book.

Tabitha's Superhero Story

... Emma's house. 'Why are we here?' they said.
'OK I think I know why,' said Ben.
'Why?' said Emma.
'Because there's a robber! We can't let him get away,' said Ben.
As soon as the robber saw them he quickly dashed into the sun.
When the two superheroes had finally caught the robber, they brought him to the police
station. They snatched all the money he had stolen and gave it to the police.
The police were very cross with the robber as he had robbed many houses before. The superheroes locked him up in jail.
'No more robbing for you!' shouted the police.
'Thank you for catching him. I would like to award you with these medals.'
So the two superheroes and their super dog flew to the magic tree and opened the door to see what villain they would be dealing with next.

Tabitha Selby-Boothroyd (7)
Danson Primary School, Welling

Lyla-Grace's Space Story

Once, there lived a girl called Emma and a boy called Ben. They found a magic door. They opened it and all of a sudden they were in... space. They adored space, they were so very, very curious. They arrived super-duper early, at like 3 o'clock. They saw an alien, they went to sleep because they didn't know what to do. They were excited that they saw their very first alien.

The alien was in a ship. Emma and Ben were underneath it with their puppy. They adored her and she was so very adorable, they didn't know what to do. The puppy adored Ben and Emma. They got in the spaceship with the silly, funny, green, slimy, kind alien and had a good old laugh and a good old bit of fun, and had a good old time and they thought that the alien was naughty.

They got out of the spaceship and they got back in and they got eaten by a mean, slimy, horrid and not adorable monster. Three-eyed, eight-legged, he was ugly, vicious and so, so, very, very, very greedy. At last they got back home safe and sound.

They were OK back where they belonged. At least the alien got away from the monster.

They were terrified at first but they weren't at the end. Also they got home very late at night or very early in the morning.

Lyla-Grace Ruby Mehmet (7)
Belvedere Infant School, Belvedere

Talha's Space Story

... space. They floated around space and they didn't get their space boots.

Ben said. 'Ha ha, I've got some spare.'

Emma said, 'Thanks, let's look around.'

Suddenly, an alien caught them and he wanted to kill them. He climbed on the stars but it didn't work, they hid behind the spaceship, and the alien was lost.

He saw them. He said, 'Stop I'm just trying to help you.'

He got them onto his flying saucer and took them away, then they landed on the moon.

They were so excited that they scared the alien. They were talking but the alien said they shouldn't talk there. 'The monster will wake up.'

Ben and Emma stopped talking.

The monster woke up and tried to kill them. He nearly killed them. But the alien flew to the magic door.

When they got out of the magic door they said sorry and said goodbye to the alien.

Talha Amzad (7)
Belvedere Infant School, Belvedere

Lucas' Space Story

The amazement the children were in! Emma and Ben said, 'That is amazing!' The dog barked at an alien, but Ben and Emma didn't care.

A cheeky green alien started squirting stinky cheese.

Ben, Emma and Dog said, 'Hello.'

The dog said, 'Woof!'

The alien jumped into his space saucer and sucked up the children and the dog. As the dog went up he went upside down.

The alien took the children on an adventure.

The children and the dog were excited. The alien was happy because the children were there.

It is night-time now because it is dark. On their adventure they saw a big, sloppy, gloopy monster with a long tongue.

They went home. When they got home it was bedtime. They brushed their teeth, got their pyjamas on and went to bed.

Lucas Suter (6)

Belvedere Infant School, Belvedere

5

Layla's Space Story

... a glorious place.

'It is space,' 'they said.

'Wow!' Emma said.

They floated to the moon and bounced on the moon.

They were touching the stars.

An alien was giggling behind them. What was the alien going to do?

When they were bouncing and jumping, something lifted them up. They saw it was an alien spaceship!

'Oh no, what should we do?'

Actually the alien was a friendly alien. The alien took them for a ride.

'The alien's spaceship is amazing!' said Ben.

When the alien was giving them a lift home, a monster attacked the space rocket. They all got very, very frightened and worried. But
they escaped the monster.

The alien took them back to where they were before.

Layla Ong (6)
Belvedere Infant School, Belvedere

Zachary's Superhero Story

The superheroes called Ben and Emma went inside a door and it took them to a beautiful world, but someone was looking for trouble. 'Now the money is mine I can go to my secret hideout, ha ha ha!'
Ben said, 'He took all the money from the bank.'
They grabbed him. 'Got you! Put your hands up in the air. You're going to prison.'
'My plan has failed. They always win, you rats!'
They locked the cage.
'Boo, hoo, hoo (crying) it's not fair. Get me out of here, please. I'll do anything.'
He broke out of prison but Emma and Ben caught him. 'Got you, you're going back to prison for good.'
The mayor gave them medals, then they went through the magic door and they went home.

Zachary Derry (6)
Belvedere Infant School, Belvedere

Barnabas' Space Story

... space. It was really dark, they could see but not too well. They saw shining bright things, but they didn't know what they were.

Then Ben was touching the stars. They were looking at the bright yellow things. They were only looking at the stars, so didn't notice that there was an alien behind them.

Later the alien dragged them up to the ship by using a pulse of green light, they didn't know what was happening.

Then they noticed that the alien was actually nice, so they went with him.

When they passed a planet they saw an ugly monster that was trying to get the ship to the ground.

After two hours the alien brought them back home with their dog. He said bye to all of them.

Barnabas Bakos (7)
Belvedere Infant School, Belvedere

Jasleen's Magical Story

... a magical land.

'Cool, there's a castle, I wonder what is there.'

On the other side there was a fairy sitting on top of a toadstool.

The dog barked at the fairy. The fairy said, 'I will give you two wishes.'

Their wishes were to have a party and eat candy.

Out came a monster. 'Hello,' said the monster.

'Come on, let's go inside the cottage.'

When they got there, there was candy. The dog licked the candy.

The monster said, 'Let's have a party!'

'Yes!' said the children.

It was late, then the children and the dog said goodbye and off they went. The children said, 'Wow! That was really fun.'

Jasleen Sandhu (7)
Belvedere Infant School, Belvedere

Vinnie-Joe's Space Story

... space. Ben was amazed. 'How did we get here?' he said.

Emma said, 'It is a magic door.'

'Yes,' said Ben.

Then they met a cheeky, green, friendly alien.

'Hello my name is Blib,' said the alien. 'Follow me please,' said Blib.

Then they began to fly in a flying saucer.

They went to save a greedy, ugly, bad monster.

Then he said, 'Go away now!'

They said, 'We're going to save you.'

'I don't want to be saved.'

'OK then,' said the alien.

'Bye-bye,' said the alien.

'I like space,' said Ben.

'I like it too,' said Emma.

Vinnie-Joe Fagan (7)
Belvedere Infant School, Belvedere

Lucas' Superhero Story

... Superhero Land. Emma and Ben heard a burglar was on the run. When Emma and Ben caught up to the burglar, then they hit a car.

'There is the burglar!' shouted Emma and Ben. 'He is stealing the bag with all of the cash. We have to stop him stealing the bag of cash.'

When they got him, he did give the cash back, they lost him because they looked back and he was on the run again. They got him back.

Because he gave the cash back, Emma and Ben saved the day.

When they were safe, the burglar smashed out of prison and said, 'Oh yeah!'

Emma and Ben went back through the tree.

Lucas Suter (6)

Belvedere Infant School, Belvedere

Annastasi's Superhero Story

... the train track. They didn't like it because it was dark there.

The baddie took the money from the goodies.

When he got the money, he spat bubblegum, it got bigger.

They saw the baddie. They took the money from the baddie and he grabbed the dog.

'Give me my dog,' shouted Emma.

The dog kicked the bad guy in the face, and then threw pies at him, until he fell into jail and turned into a pancake.

The police gave them a massive chocolate bunny and medals because they saved the day.

The baddie escaped from jail. Emma and Ben followed him through the magic tree to a castle. The baddie used a tornado to blow the castle up.

Annastasi Zan-Bi-Nation (6)
Belvedere Infant School, Belvedere

Cody's Superhero Story

... a magic Ninja Master World that was full of ninjas. They were shooting Ninja stars at Emma and Ben.

They saw a robber at the shop who was shouting, 'Give me all your money.'

The robber ran away with all the money.

Emma used her powers to freeze the floor and the robber slipped over. Barker used his mega-bark to help Ben catch the robber.

Emma and Ben put the robber in jail. 'Get me out of here!' he shouted.

The police gave Emma, Ben and Barker all medals for catching the robber.

They went back through the magic door and landed in a world made of gold.

Cody Wiecek (6)

Belvedere Infant School, Belvedere

Honey-Rae's Superhero Story

One day it was light and Emma and Ben flew in the blue sky.

'It is a sunny day today.' They flew with their dog
The robber took the cash. The robber has a black mask. he was laughing, he was stealing money. The robber ran away to a hideout.

The superheroes saw the robber and said, 'Stop there! You're going down, you're going to jail.'

He was sad because he was in jail. He was not really happy.

The heroes got a badge. They had saved the day. They all went back to the magic door. It was a good day. It was a funny day.

Honey-Rae Williams (6)
Belvedere Infant School, Belvedere

Tommy's Space Story

... space. Emma and Ben were amazed about it. They were holding hands and Emma was holding her dog as well.

When Emma and Ben were putting stars in the dark, ebony, sky, an alien saw them. He spied on them.

The alien captured Emma and Ben and Emma's dog, and they got in the flying saucer.

The alien was friends with Ben and Emma, so they played all day.

Until the space monster saw them playing. He was annoyed because they were friends, so he tried to get home.

Then they got back to the magic door.

Tommy Nicholls Aird (7)
Belvedere Infant School, Belvedere

Alice's Jungle Story

... a jungle. Emma and Ben were walking the dog. They saw lots of leaves on long trees.

They saw a red and yellow snake, the dog put his tongue on the snake.

The snake ran after Ben and Emma. They had to run as fast as they could. They were out of breath. They met a tall lion. They said, 'Can you give us a lift?'

'Yes,' said the lion.

The lion ran as fast as he could to the magic door. They had to walk a bit.

When they got there, they opened the door and went back to their lovely home.

Alice Elizabeth Brooks (7)
Belvedere Infant School, Belvedere

Aniq's Superhero Story

... Superhero Land. Then they were in the costumes of superheroes, but then they caught a robber red-handed.

'Stop right there!' said Ben. 'Drop that bag.'

He dropped the bag.

Emma said, 'I'm calling the police.'

The dog was barking.

'No police will come!'

Suddenly, they appeared. The police had come and they took the robber to jail.

Emma and Ben said, 'Yes!' and high-fived.

They went home with badges. They went through the magic door and went home.

Aniq Olorunteleola Okin (5)

Belvedere Infant School, Belvedere

Pavandeep's Superhero Story

Ben and Emma were flying in the sky. 'Let's have a fly with the dog.'

There was a bang. It was a robber. The robber was running fast.

'Stop that!' said Ben. So the robber stopped. 'Give that money to the bank. Now you have to go to jail.'

'I will never be a robber again,' and the robber was crying.

'Look, we've got a medal and we saved the day!'

'I need to go home.' Ben and Emma went home, and they were excited.

Pavandeep Singh Dhesi (6)
Belvedere Infant School, Belvedere

Emanuela's Superhero Story

... the castle. The castle was colourful. The castle was huge. They liked the colours.

Emma and Ben saw a bad guy running from the castle. He had stolen the king's money.

They grabbed the bad guy and said, 'Stealing is bad.'

They took him to jail and locked him in, and gave the keys to the police.

The king gave Emma and Ben a gold medal each. They were excited. The dog got a medal as well and a bone.

They all went back to the tree and they went back home.

Emanuela Ciobanu (6)

Belvedere Infant School, Belvedere

Jemima's Space Story

One sunny day, Emma and Ben saw a cheeky alien.
They walked closer and closer until...
He took them to a special place that no one knew.
When they got there they saw beautiful stars.
Then a big, ugly monster tried to take them back
home.
He was just about to take them home but...
There was a giant monster. He tried to get them
but they survived.
The friendly alien managed to take them back
home.
They said, 'Wow, what an adventure!'

Jemima Oyeneye (7)
Belvedere Infant School, Belvedere

Nifemi's Superhero Story

... Superhero World, and Ben was Super-Ben and Emma was Super-Emma. They were soaring through the sky.

Suddenly, they spotted a robber. They thought he'd robbed a bank. So they zoomed down to catch the bad robber.

When they reached him, they grabbed the bag with $1,000,000.

They called the cops to take him away and put him in jail.

Because of their good work they all got a prize including their dog.

So they all flew back home.

Nifemi Ayorinde-Salami (7)
Belvedere Infant School, Belvedere

Joshua's Space Story

On the other side there were tiny stars everywhere.
Ben and Emma and the dog all knew they were
floating in space.
Behind them there was a nasty, mean alien,
laughing when Ben and Emma were looking at
the tiny stars.
Suddenly, the alien's flying saucer sucked up
Emma and Ben, also the dog.
The alien gave all of them a ride on his spaceship.
Under the ship was an ugly monster that was very
huge.
The alien gave them a ride back home.

Joshua Ayibatin (8)
Belvedere Infant School, Belvedere

Lola's Space Story

... space. When they went in the magic door they thought it was a miracle.

Ben and Emma were standing on the grey moon.

Ben touched the light of a shining star,

Suddenly a shocking, shining thing came out of the sky.

When they got inside they realised that it was an alien ship, but they became friends with the alien.

Suddenly, they felt a lick on the ship.

When they got out they waved at the alien and they went back home.

Lola Stroud (7)

Belvedere Infant School, Belvedere

Jessica's Superhero Story

... a magic silver castle and in the sliver castle there was lots of silver and gold money.

A villain called Vicky stole the gold and silver money that was in the silver castle.

Emma and Ben said, 'Hey! Stop there Vicky, we're going to put you in jail!'

'Why am I in jail? Why was I bad? I wish I was good.'

'I'm so happy, we got the medals!'

'I am happy too.'

'Come on Emma, let's go to walk the dog.'

Jessica Kainth (6)
Belvedere Infant School, Belvedere

Layla's Superhero Story

... Thunderland. In Thunderland, it's cold and dark.
Emma and Ben were worried.
Suddenly, Eden the robber was in Thunderland.
Eden was not worried. Not worried at all.
Eden said, 'No, you're scared!'
They grabbed him, he wiggled and jiggled to escape, he couldn't escape though.
He was in prison, he couldn't get out.
They called the police to get him into prison.
That's why they won medals.
They went back home.

Layla Allia Bestford (6)
Belvedere Infant School, Belvedere

Dixie's Superhero Story

... a Wonder World, and then Dum Boy stole a special crown.

'There Dum Boy is,' said Ben. 'Dum Boy come here.'

'Dum Boy you are completely stuck in jail.'

'Dum Boy, why are you so mean?'

'Why?' said Ben and Emma.

'Woof!' said Simon.

'You are crazy!' said Ben and Emma.

The door was still there. 'Should we go back in the door?'

'No way,' said Ben.

Dixie Ellis Wainwright (6)

Belvedere Infant School, Belvedere

Zahra's Superhero Story

Then the door took them into Rainbow World. All the places there were colourful. Instantly they saw a robber robbing the bank, and then he ran into his secret hideout. 'Mwahahaha! All of the money is mine, all mine!'

The superheroes cornered the robber and then they put him in jail.

The robber cried and he said, 'I will get you next time.'

Then the superheroes saved the day!

Emma said, 'Let's go home.'

Zahra Gerasimova (6)
Belvedere Infant School, Belvedere

Ryan's Superhero Story

... the clouds. They turned into superheroes in the sunny sky and they saw a bad guy.

The bad guy had stolen the jewels from the church so the superheroes were cross with the robber. The superheroes caught the bad guy and now he is sad because he is in jail.

'We saved the day!' Emma and Ben are happy because they were awarded medals.

The superheroes saw the magic door and they flew through the magic door.

Ryan Xuereb (6)
Belvedere Infant School, Belvedere

Lucas' Superhero Story

... the sky. Emma and Ben went through a secret door in a tree, they opened the door.

A burglar stole some cash from the bank. Emma and Ben had to save the day.

Emma and Ben got him. 'If you don't hand over the cash you will go in prison.'

When he was in prison he said, 'No! No! No! I am in prison!'

Emma and Ben saved the day.

Emma and Ben then got out of there.

Lucas Shane Hawkins (8)

Belvedere Infant School, Belvedere

Kayden's Superhero Story

... Superhero Land. They turned into superheroes and they saw the magic door. But they
didn't stay in Superhero Land.
They saw a robber. He stole some money from a bank.
'You're not going anywhere,' said Ben.
'They put the robber in jail. Moping, he went there.
They both got a rosette, so did the dog.
On their way home they spotted the magic door.

Kayden Eve (6)
Belvedere Infant School, Belvedere

Ethan's Space Story

... space. Emma and Ben were on an adventure.
Ben caught a star and an alien was watching
them.
The alien had a plan to become friend with Emma
and Ben.
The alien said, 'Can I be your friend?'
They said, 'OK.' So they let him be their friend.
A big, gigantic space alien attacked the alien ship.
They said bye-bye and the alien blasted off
in three, two, one, zero!

Ethan Williams-Smith (7)

Belvedere Infant School, Belvedere

Ty'ree's Superhero Story

It took them to Superhero Land. Just then, they saw the robber.

'The money's mine, ha ha ha. I'm going to my secret hideout.'

'Give us our money back.'

'No!' said the robber.

'Jail. Back in jail,' said the robber, and he cried.

Emma and Ben and the dog got badges from the Mayor.

'I see the magic door.'

They lived happily ever after.

Ty'ree Zan-Bi-Nation (6)

Belvedere Infant School, Belvedere

Joseph's Space Story

It took them to space, they saw a rocket. Inside the rocket there were some aliens.

They were amazed. Ben said, 'Wow!' The aliens were very kind.

The aliens took them to the planet they lived on. The aliens put them in their rocket.

Suddenly an ugly monster came. They drove away from the monster.

The alien took them back home. Emma and Ben said, 'Thank you very much.'

Joseph Emmanuel (7)
Belvedere Infant School, Belvedere

Khushi's Superhero Story

They flew up into the sunny, blue sky and then
turned into superheroes.
Rufus took money from the bank and he was
happy that he had stolen it.
'Put your hands up!' said the superheroes.
'You're going to jail.'
Rufus was sad, he didn't like jail.
The superheroes won medals from the Mayor.
They went home. They lived happily ever after.

Khushi Bajwa (7)
Belvedere Infant School, Belvedere

Lilie's Superhero Story

... the sky. They were flying in the blue sky.

They saw a villain! 'Come back here!' said Emma. He had a black mask and a black hat.

'Drop that down,' said Emma and Ben. Then they took the bag off him.

They went to prison. He felt sad.

Then they got a badge from the queen. They felt so excited.

So they went through the magic door back home.

Lilie El Kedhri (5)

Belvedere Infant School, Belvedere

Maximus' Superhero Story

Ben and Emma were in the light blue sky. Ben and Emma saw a robber. The robber was running with the money.

Ben said, 'Stop right there!'

'You can't get me!' said the robber but was caught. The robber went to prison. 'My plan is ruined.'

Ben and Emma saved the day. Ben saw the tree and they went back home.

Maximus Scott (6)
Belvedere Infant School, Belvedere

Aimee's Superhero Story

... a world full of flowers.

It was hot. Suddenly, they saw a robber.

'Ha ha ha! Nobody can stop me,' he said.

'Stop right there! Grab him. You aren't going anywhere.'

'My plan has failed, you fools!'

'We saved the day!'

'That was fun. It was magic.'

Aimee Charlotte Garrard-Dinnadge (6)
Belvedere Infant School, Belvedere

Our Superhero Story

... the clouds. They turned into superheroes and they were flying in the sky.

The bad guy robbed the bank and stole the money.

'Stop right there!' Emma and Ben caught the bad guy.

'You ruined my plan.'

We saved the day again.

They saw the magic door.

Amber Grace Micetich (6) & Henry

Belvedere Infant School, Belvedere

Prabhbir's Superhero Story

They turned into superheroes and they were
flying in the sky.
The bad guy robbed the bank and stole the money.
'Stop right there! We caught the bad guy.'
Then he was under arrest.
They got badges.
They went home.

Prabhbir Singh Atwal (6)
Belvedere Infant School, Belvedere

Georgie's Space Story

... space. They opened the magic door.
They saw an alien on the moon.
They got taken by an alien.
They were friends with the alien.
The alien was trying to eat them.
They went back home to their mum and dad.

Georgie Lynn Hanscombe (7)
Belvedere Infant School, Belvedere

Logan's Superhero Story

They turned into superheroes and flew in the sky.
They saw a bad guy.
'Stop right there!' said Emma and Ben and they caught the bad guy. 'You're under arrest!'
They got medals.
They went home.

Logan Collis (6)
Belvedere Infant School, Belvedere

Layla's Magical Story

... a castle. Inside the castle there was a fairy
princess called Periwinkle.
Ben and Emma said, 'Hello,'
And the dog barked, 'Hello.'
Periwinkle said, 'Hello,' too but
something was wrong.
'What's the matter, Periwinkle?'
'There is a big monster trying to catch me.'
'I'll see what I can do.'
'Wait, I'll go with you.'
'OK.' Ben and Emma replied. 'Come on, let's go.'
'W-w-who are are you?'
'I am Ben.'
'And I am Emma.'
So Emma and Ben and Periwinkle followed a troll
called Snow As A Wos. Snow As A Wos said,
'Should we have a party?'
'OK but only if we make friends.'
So they all made decorations, except for
Patrick the dog. Patrick was excited for the party,
and nobody else came.

They got their presents and their stuff and went home. They told their mum and dad all about it. 'It started with a castle...'

Layla Doris Ward (6)
Danson Primary School, Welling

Sophia's Pirate Story

... a beautiful, flowery forest. They saw a canoe and rowed it to an island.

They had a big bump when they got to the island. Then to their surprise they saw 'X marks the Spot.'

They dug and dug until they found a chest.

They opened it.

Then they found treasure in it.

A little while later, a pirate slung out his sword and said, 'Give me that golden treasure!' He took the chest, children and puppy.

An hour later they sailed across the vast ocean on a clear setting. He told them all, including the dog, to walk the plank into the deep sea.

So they had to do it, otherwise they would have to do it another way.

Scared they jumped but luckily the dolphins caught them and took them to the magic tree.

Then they got on land and started running to the tree, but on the way there they met a serpent, quickly they became friends and went home.

Sophia McAvoy (7)

Danson Primary School, Welling

Charlotte's Space Story

... space. They were shocked! They saw lots of beautiful stars around them.

When they looked around again they saw that they were on a planet. Behind them stood a large, green, big-eyed alien. They were really scared! They were just about to walk off the moon when they got sucked up by the alien's spaceship. They wondered where it would take them.

By the time they got sucked up by the alien's spaceship, they found out that the alien was actually really, really, really friendly, he was taking them to his home.

On their way back home with the alien, they nearly got sucked up by a monster. The monster had three eyes and nine legs. He was so scary!

When the alien dropped the girl, the boy and the dog off, they said, 'Thank you for taking us on a beautiful trip'. After that, they walked back to their tree house.

Charlotte Galbraith (7)
Danson Primary School, Welling

Mai's Magical Story

... a step into a new land. When they were on the other side of the door, they saw a magical castle, so they started to walk over to it. As they were walking over to it, they saw a glittering fairy sitting on a mushroom.

'What is your name?' asked the children.

'My name is...'

'Her name is Tinkerbell! She is one of the magical fairies and I'm the Candy Troll.' The troll smelt of chocolate.

'Well, I am Emma and this is Ben, my brother. We are here as when we were playing fetch with our dog, we came across a magical door.'

It was the troll's birthday, so they had a party in his candy cane house, and they had lots of cake. At the end of the party they went back through the magic door and all lived happily ever after.

Mai Poppy Greenhead (7)
Danson Primary School, Welling

Aarush's Jungle Story

... a jungle! Emma was a bit scared but Ben wasn't.
'Let's swing on these vines,' said Ben. They had lots
of fun.

Then they met a snake. He thought the snake was
friendly, but he wasn't.

'Hello and I want to eat you!' said the snake.

Emma and Ben were scared. Emma and Ben ran
faster and faster until the snake was nowhere near
them.

Then Emma and Ben met a lion. 'Hello Mr Lion, can
you help us to find our way home?' they said.

'I'd love to help you,' said Mr Lion.

Emma and Ben went off to go home.

'Mr Lion, please can we get off?' Ben said.

They swung on vines until Emma and Ben saw the
magic door. They had a lot of fun.

Aarush Devalpalli (6)
Danson Primary School, Welling

Finley's Magical Story

... a magical land. On the other side was a big scary hill when they saw a fort. A big scary monster lived in there.

But a tiny fairy went on a mushroom. She had pink sparkly wings. She wanted them to be knights for her castle.

Then a goblin said, 'Hello!'

They were surprised!

The goblin said, 'Do you want to come to my party?'

They said yes, and set up the decorations and food, and the dog found the presents and they gave them to the dog.

They all had a party in the goblin's house and celebrated. It was nearly time to go, so they left. When they left they talked about the goblin's house. 'It was small, smelly and rubbish!'

Finley Penney (6)

Danson Primary School, Welling

Balpreet's Space Story

... space! Emma and Ben were shocked with what they saw. The sky was pitch-black and the stars were shining like diamonds.

A small alien noticed them wondering.

While they were exploring, the alien brought his spaceship and planned to capture them. He slowly pulled them up with his gravity.

Emma, Ben and the dog were very happy to be in the spaceship. They were all very excited.

A monster came along and tried to capture them. Everyone started to panic, however the alien was smart and turned the ship around.

The alien felt that Emma, Ben and the dog would be safe back home so he dropped them off where they belonged.

Balpreet Kaur Sangar (6)
Danson Primary School, Welling

Michael's Pirate Story

... to a pirate island. They were on a really small boat and a small island, it was very sunny.
They even found treasure and they were shocked. Ben was shocked, Emma was happy, their dog barked, he was joyful.
A scruffy old pirate came. 'Oh shiver me timbers, that's me treasure!'
'No it's not!'
'Oh yes it is. Arrr!' said the pirate.
The pirate took them on his ship and told them to walk the plank. They were scared...
They jumped and they landed on dolphins then got away. They were so joyful and happy.
They went back to the tree. They all lived happily ever after.

Michael Inioluwa Hassan (7)
Danson Primary School, Welling

Luca's Superhero Story

... the bottom of the ocean! They saw a blue whale that squirted some water and treasure out!

They also spotted a burglar trying to steal some shiny treasure. They watched him for a minute to see if he was a real burglar.

He was! 'What were you doing?' said Emma.

The burglar said, 'I'm stealing the treasure.'

Emma and Ben decided to put him in jail, so he can learn his lesson. The burglar felt worried and Ben and Emma felt safe.

They felt chuffed because they got medals for their bravery. Even the dog got a medal!

Finally they went back to the tree to go home and told everyone about their experience.

Luca Blake (6)

Danson Primary School, Welling

Penelope's Pirate Story

... the sea. It was a sunny day, it was so fresh. They were sailing then they saw a light, it was bright like the sun. They pushed the boat to a desert island, then found the glowing light, it was a treasure chest.

A ship came along, the ship had pirates on it. The captain pirate rowed over to the island and he said, 'It is my treasure, it doesn't belong to you.' The captain pirate captured them and took them to the ship. He tied them up and made them walk the plank.

When they got in the sea, two dolphins came and they helped them to escape.

They ran back home to their mum and dad and told them about the pirates.

Penelope Hynes (6)
Danson Primary School, Welling

Lucy's Jungle Story

... the jungle. Emma and Ben were swinging on long ropes with their pet dog Badger. They were in the jungle.

'Then they got off the rope and they saw a huge snake.

He hissed at them and said, 'I'm hungry!' Then the snake chased them and they ran as fast as they could.

Then they saw a lion and he said, 'I like your pet dog.'

They played with the lion and played hide-and-seek. Then they rode on his back.

Then they swung on the ropes back to the tree, with the secret door that took them home. What an adventure!

Lucy Horne (6)
Danson Primary School, Welling

Brooke's Magical Story

... a fairy-tale forest! They saw a beautiful, pretty, pink and red fairy castle.

Inside they found a colourful fairy. The fairy said, 'Hello, are you gong to go to the party?'

Yes,' said Emma and Ben.

Afterwards they found a smelly troll.

He said, 'Hello, I'm called Stinky, because I'm stinky.'

Next he told them the way to the exciting party.

'Its thirty-six lefts and then you'll see it on the right.'

They did that and had fun. They had fun forever. Finally they went home.

Brooke Perring (6)

Danson Primary School, Welling

Cali's Superhero Story

... Superhero Land. It was a sunny day and Emma and Ben were training their dog Penny.

But there was a robber called Rob and he robbed the bank and he put it in a sack.

Emma and Ben saw Rob and he was scared! 'What are you doing?' said Emma.

'I am going to put you in jail for sixty weeks and you will not escape prison.'

Emma and Ben walked down a little mountain and walked the dog.

Ben and Emma locked the doors really tight, so Rob couldn't escape.

Cali Cato (7)

Danson Primary School, Welling

Archie's Pirate Story

... a golden, sandy beach where they found a wooden ship which they sailed on the sea.

After many days they saw a small island with a chest full of yummy chocolate coins.

Suddenly, they saw a pirate with a black hat, but then he said, 'Walk the plank!'

Their bodies shook into the cold water. *Splash!* they were wet.

Emma called her dolphin friends and went for a ride.

They got home safely.

Archie Mark Berry (5)
Danson Primary School, Welling

Ryan's Superhero Story

There was a beautiful house in a tree. Emma and Ben were walking their dogs nearby. They noticed the house door was broken. When they reached inside the house to check, they saw a burglar running with a sack full of money.

They caught the burglar and called the police. The police jailed the burglar. The police thanked Emma and Ben.

They continued to walk their dog.

Ryan Poudel (6)

Danson Primary School, Welling

Daisy's Magical Story

... a land with a golden castle.

The castle had a glittery roof and yellow walls. Emma, Ben and Emma's dog went into the castle to see who lived there.

They found a magical fairy. She was upset because she lost her shoes, which were special. They were supposed to take her to her birthday party. Ben was shocked.

There was a smelly old troll behind them. 'Don't worry, I will help,' said the troll. 'I can take you to the birthday party.' Ben and Emma were not sure but they followed the troll.

The troll took them to the gingerbread man's house. It had icing on the roof and it was made of biscuits.

When they went inside they saw balloons, cakes and hats. They all danced and the fairy was the best dancer. The troll had lots of presents.

After the exciting party, Emma and Ben went home. The dog stayed with the troll to help keep him company.

Daisy Deal (6)
Drapers Mills Primary Academy, Margate

Tiffany's Magical Story

... Troll Land. They were surprised. They wanted to go back to the tree.

Suddenly, a fairy came. 'Stop!' she said. 'Don't go there, you will die!'

'Where should we go?'

'Follow me, I will show you.'

They saw a weird troll. He said, 'How are you? I'm really a person. A wizard turned me into a troll. Do you want to come to my party?'

'Yes!' they said. So they followed him.

What is this?'

'It's a party!'

'Yay!'

They had party food, then they had to go.

They brought some nice presents back home.

Tiffany Shannon (6)

Drapers Mills Primary Academy, Margate

Danielius' Magical Story

... a castle.

Next, a fairy came, she said, 'Do not enter, there are trolls and they're unkind.'

They entered anyway.

Then Emma and Ben saw a magical smelly and fat troll. Emma and Ben were so scared.

After that, the troll took Emma and Ben to his house. The dog licked the candy and they saw the gingerbread house.

They had a party, they were so happy. They had presents and balloons and party food.

At the end Emma and Ben needed to go home. They were given presents and party food.

Danielius Juscuis (6)

Drapers Mills Primary Academy, Margate

Ethan's Magical Story

They opened the magic door, they were shocked, they saw a castle.

They found a fairy too, she said they mustn't go in the castle. They saw a troll, it was smelly and furry. The troll said, 'You can come to my party.'

The children ate some cake.

They had to go back home.

Ethan Rattray (6)

Drapers Mills Primary Academy, Margate

Ewan's Jungle Story

... a jungle and they were swinging on vines!
Then they saw a snake curled up. They were scared.

They ran away from the snake as fast as they could.

Next they saw a lion. Then they thought it was going to eat them!

But it was nice. Then it gave them a ride.

Then they swung on the vines back to the magic door. Then they went home.

Ewan Murphy (6)
Finberry Primary School, Ashford

Rose's Superhero Story

... where there was a secret garden. They ran to the bad man.

The bad man had lots of stolen coins in his bag.

The children shouted, 'Stop!'

The bad man stopped and Emma and Ben looked at the bad man and told him off.

They put him in jail.

Then Ben and Emma and the dog were rewarded.

They flew back to the secret door and went back home.

Rose Eliana Finn (5)

Finberry Primary School, Ashford

Jessica's Superhero Story

... a beautiful palace. Inside was a dressing up box. They changed into superheroes.
A burglar came and knocked down the palace with a hammer.
The children said, 'No, stop!' to the baddie.
They put him in jail.
They were really happy, they got medals.
They flew back home.

Jessica Davis (5)
Finberry Primary School, Ashford

Lawk's Jungle Story

... a forest. They were swinging in the forest.

They saw a long snake.

The snake scared them and they ran away.

They met a lion. They were scared of the lion, but he was kind.

The lion helped them get out.

Then they played happily in the forest.

Lawk Abdulkareem (6)

Finberry Primary School, Ashford

Tyler's Superhero Story

In the bedroom there was a magic hat and a
rabbit came out.
A baddy stole money from the bank to spend it.
Toby found them.
They put him in jail.
What a busy day.
'Look, there is a magic hat!'

Tyler Gardiner
Finberry Primary School, Ashford

Nshira's Jungle Story

... a jungle. They swung on a rope.
They saw a snake.
They were running from the snake.
Then they saw a lion.
The lion took them back home.
Ben and Emma swung on a rope again.

Nshira Yaw Preko (6)
Finberry Primary School, Ashford

Lilly's Magical Story

... a lovely, giant and white castle with three flags poking out on the top of the lovely castle and a wooden door.

Emma and Ben opened the magic door and they saw a tiny fairy sitting on a big mushroom. Then a big, fat, smelly and hairy monster with flies flying around it appeared. Emma and Ben held their noses.

After, they built a giant gingerbread house with candy canes, icing, cutters, heart cutters and more cutters.

Then Emma and Ben and the dog set up a party for the smelly monster.

Afterwards Emma and Ben went home with cake, hats, presents and a balloon each.

Lilly Davies (6)

Horizon Primary Academy, Swanley

Untitled

... a bad beach with monkeys, bad ones, that put them in deep water and laughed at them.

Then a boat was in the middle of the ocean. On the boat were two pirates and they said, 'Hop on my boat matey!'

Then the pirates tied Emma and Ben up to their post. It is really called a flag.

The poor little dog couldn't swim in the ocean, he got tied up as well.

He yelped, 'Help! Help!' Some fairy just appeared out of nowhere.

The pirates went to a desert. They made it!

Tasanee Lamai Purser (6)

Horizon Primary Academy, Swanley

Deborah's Magical Story

... a magic castle. Emma, Ben and the dog were really surprised.

When they were walling past, they met a fairy sitting on a mushroom and Emma and Ben stopped.

Then Emma and Ben saw a stinky, disgusting troll, The puppy thought the troll was disgusting.

Next, the troll took the them to a candy house.

Emma and Ben had a birthday party and they had fun.

Finally they went home happily, but they had a party.

Deborah Teniola Adeyemi (6)
Horizon Primary Academy, Swanley

70

Untitled

It led them to a happy-looking school.

They opened the door and then they went into a hallway, and it was filled with fairies.

They saw an upstairs and they went upstairs and saw loads of fairies.

There were loads of them because it was their school.

The teacher fairy came and saw them and came to them to see what they were doing.

It was time to go home, then they found the tree and got out.

Lily Bassett (6)
Horizon Primary Academy, Swanley

Katherine's Magical Story

... a castle that had a pathway up to it and had three flags.

They found a fairy and the fairy and the dog were barking.

The dog saw a troll and the troll was very stinky.

The troll showed Emma and Ben his house, and the house was beautiful.

And Emma and Ben could fit through the little door and they had a party.

Then they went back home.

Katherine Sophie Faith Jefferys (6)
Horizon Primary Academy, Swanley

Prince's Space Story

... space. Emma and Ben were on the moon. They were having a good time, but there was a sneaky alien, he was little.

They got sucked in. But the alien was friendly. When they were flying there was a big monster, the monster grabbed onto the ship.

The ship crashed onto Planet Earth. Emma and Ben said, 'Bye! Come again soon.'

The alien said, 'I will.'

Prince Hopkins (6)
Horizon Primary Academy, Swanley

Kieran's Space Story

... space. They were flying around the world.
Suddenly, they landed on the moon of rock, but an alien looked at Emma and Ben.
The alien got in the flying saucer and he sucked up Emma and Ben.
They were friends forever and ever.
A big alien called Chris appeared and licked them but they got away.
They said goodbye to the alien.

Kieran Duffey (5)

Horizon Primary Academy, Swanley

Untitled

... a witch that had magical powers. Emma and Ben ran. Ben hid and Emma hid. The witch went back.

They got out of a tree, they ran away from the tree.

Emma and Ben saw the witch.The witch ran at them.

Ben got grabbed by the witch.

Ben escaped from the witch. The witch was angry.

The witch fell asleep.

Ella Stephens (5)

Horizon Primary Academy, Swanley

Brandon's Magical Story

... a magical place.

Then they met a fairy and an ugly beast.

And then they met a monster, that was smelly.

And he showed his house to them.

And he held a party.

And they went home.

Brandon Lampard (6)

Horizon Primary Academy, Swanley

George's Magical Story

... a castle.

That day they went on a walk.

Then they met a fairy.

Then they met a troll.

Then he helped them.

Then they had a party.

Then they went home.

George Benjamin Hughes (6)

Horizon Primary Academy, Swanley

Sienna's Jungle Story

... a dark, scary jungle. They began to swing on the vines and they felt happy,

'This is fun!' shouted Ben and Emma.

All of a sudden, they bumped into an angry, sly snake! The snake hissed, 'I'm going to eat you!'

So Emma and Ben ran as fast as their little legs could carry them and the snake was hissing behind them. The snake was fast, but it still didn't catch them.

Suddenly, from out of the bushes a lion popped out. Ben and Emma were very frightened. The lion said, 'Hello.'

Ben and Emma jumped.

He said, 'What's the matter?'

'We can't get back home.'

'Don't worry,' said the lion, 'hop onto my back.'

So Emma and Ben hopped onto the lion's back. The lion took Emma and Ben to their home. Emma and Ben were very excited to tell their parents their story and they did.

Sienna Jaina Dhiraj (6)
Lawley Primary School, Lawley

Tegan's Space Story

... space! Emma and Ben were picking golden stars and floating in space. They were happy and excited. The Earth was under them.

Suddenly, a green little alien came! They were on the moon. There were holes on the moon. Emma and Ben had sparkly white spacesuits.

Suddenly, a spaceship sucked Emma and Ben up into it. They were screaming and scared, the ship made a *swoosh* noise. It was a silver ship.

He was a kind alien after all. He just had no friends and was lonely. He zoomed with them. He told funny jokes so they played with him.

All of a sudden, an ugly monster came out then they squished him. He was a gloomy monster. They were in the park back on Earth.

The alien said, 'Bee blob,' and waved at them bye, then Emma and Ben smiled.

Tegan Walters (6)

Lawley Primary School, Lawley

Emily's Jungle Story

... a dark scary jungle. They began to swing on the green, wet vines and they felt happy. 'This is fun!' shouted Emma and Ben.

All of a sudden, they bumped into a green snake! The snake hissed, 'I'm going to eat you!'

Scared for their lives, they started to run. However the green snake didn't give up, he was getting closer and closer.

Fortunately they met a friendly lion. The lion said, 'Hello, how can I help you?'

The children cried, 'There's a scary snake chasing us, can you help us get home?'

The lion kindly replied, 'Climb onto my furry back.' The children felt very happy.

The children were delighted to find themselves back at the magic door.

Emily Harrison (6)
Lawley Primary School, Lawley

Isla's Magical Story

... an amazing land. It was Party Land! They saw a beautiful palace and they wanted to go in.

They skipped along the sparkly path. Suddenly, they saw a fairy.

'My name is Elizabeth.'

She told them a smelly ogre was taking all the sweets.

Ben and Emma found the stinky ogre. They told him the fairy was sad.

He said, 'Find my chocolate house and I will give you the sweets.'

On the way they met a talking dog who told them the way. Soon they found the delicious house and the spell was broken!

The new friends had a party. There was cake, hot dogs and music.

Eventually it was time to go. The new friends gave Ben and Emma a silver present. Finally they opened the magic door.

Isla Grace Edwards (6)
Lawley Primary School, Lawley

Daisy's Space Story

... space! Emma and Ben saw so many stars that they couldn't believe their eyes! They loved the dark, glistening space!

Emma and Ben landed on Planet Goozoge. There was a naughty, red, tiny, sneaky alien behind them. Suddenly, a gold and red spaceship came and sucked them up with a really bright light. Emma and Ben were very worried and scared.

Actually the alien was really kind. The alien wanted friends. So they all played with him because he told funny jokes.

Then a ginormous monster tried to eat them and their ship, so they used the flattening mat to squish him into a pancake.

The alien took them back to Earth and they waved a wave and the alien said, 'Die bloo.'

Daisy Godfrey (6)
Lawley Primary School, Lawley

Megan's Magical Story

... an amazing land! It was Sweetie Land. They saw a sweetie and chocolate palace and they wanted to go in. Happily they ran along the rainbow path. Suddenly, they saw a pretty sad fairy.

'My name is Lowri.'

She told them a smelly ogre was stealing sweets.

Ben and Emma found the stinky ogre. They told him the fairy was sad.

He said, 'Find my chips that are chocolate on my house, and I will give back the sweet.'

On the way they met a cheetah who told them the way. Soon they found the yummy house and the spell was broken.

The new friends had a party. There was cake, music and party hats.

Eventually it was time to go. The new friends gave Ben and Emma pretty presents. Finally they opened the magic door.

Megan Broadhead (6)

Lawley Primary School, Lawley

Lucy's Jungle Story

... a dark, scary jungle. They began to swing on the vines and they felt happy. 'This is fun!' shouted Ben and Emma.

All of a sudden, they bumped into an angry, sly snake! The sly snake hissed, 'I'm going to eat you!' Scared for their lives, they started to run. However the hungry snake didn't give up. He was getting closer and closer!

Fortunately they met a friendly lion. He said, 'Hello, how can I help you?'

The children cried, 'There is an angry snake after us, can you help us get back home?'

The lion kindly replied, 'Climb onto my furry back.' The children were delighted to find themselves back at the magic door.

Lucy Olivia Mantle (6)

Lawley Primary School, Lawley

Sam's Magical Story

... a castle. The castle had lots of colours and I went up the rainbow path. There were lots of different colours.

Suddenly, they saw a pretty, sad fairy.

'My name is Emma.' The fairy told them a smelly ogre was taking all the sweeties.

Ben and Emma found the stinky ogre. They told him the fairy was sad.

He said, 'Find my chocolate house and I will give back the sweets.'

On the way they met a talking dog who told them the way. Soon they found the yummy house and the spell was broken!

The new friends had a party. There were balloons, music and cake.

Eventually it was time to go. The new friends gave Ben and Emma gold presents. Finally they opened the magic door.

Sam Wright (6)
Lawley Primary School, Lawley

Katie's Jungle Story

... a dark, scary jungle.

They began to swing on the vines and they felt happy.

'This is fun!' shouted cool Ben and Emma.

All of a sudden, they bumped into an angry, sly snake! The sly snake hissed, 'I'm going to eat you!' Scared out of their skin, they started to run.

However the hungry snake didn't give up! He was getting closer and closer!

Fortunately they met a friendly lion. He said, 'Hello, how can I help you?'

The children cried, 'There is a mean snake after us, can you help us get home please?'

The lion kindly replied, 'Come onto my furry back.'

The children were delighted to find themselves back at the magic door.

Katie Snik (6)
Lawley Primary School, Lawley

Lily-Dee's Magical Story

... an amazing land. It was Party Land. They saw a diamond palace and they wanted to go in. Happily they ran along the rainbow path.

Suddenly, they saw a pretty fairy.

'My name is Poppy!'

She told them a smelly ogre was stealing sweets.

Ben and Emma found the stinky ogre. They told him the fairy was sad.

He said, 'Find my Haribo house and I will give back the sweets.'

On the way they met a talking rabbit who told them the way. Soon they found the tasty house and the spell was broken!

The new friends had a party! There was music, jelly and party hats.

Eventually it was time to go. The new friends gave Ben and Emma big and little presents. Finally they opened the magic door.

Lily-Dee Smith (6)
Lawley Primary School, Lawley

Archie's Jungle Story

... a dark, scary jungle. Emma and Ben were feeling happy. They were swinging on long green vines. 'This is fun!' shouted Ben.

All of a sudden, they bumped into a sly, green snake. The snake hissed, 'I'm going to eat you!'

They were scared out of their skin! They started to run. However the sly snake got closer and closer and closer!

Fortunately they met a friendly, orange lion. He said, 'How can I help you?'

'There is a long, sly, green snake chasing us. Can we ride on your back, Lion?'

'Yes of course,' the lion kindly responded, 'Yes, climb onto my furry back.'

The children were delighted to find themselves back at the magic door.

Archie Charman (7)
Lawley Primary School, Lawley

Pennie's Jungle Story

... a dark scary jungle. Soon Emma and Ben were swinging on vines and they felt happy. 'This is fun!' shouted Emma and Ben.

All of a sudden they bumped into an angry, sly snake. The humongous snake hissed, 'I'm going to eat you!'

Scared out of their wits they started to run. However the hungry snake chased the boy and girl. He got closer and closer. They felt frightened.

Fortunately they met an orange, friendly lion.

'Hello, how can I help you?'

'There is a great, big, sly snake behind us.'

The kind lion replied, 'Jump onto my back.'

They felt very happy.

The children were delighted to find themselves at the magic door and they went home.

Pennie Rose Whitehouse (6)

Lawley Primary School, Lawley

Mia's Magical Story

... an amazing land. It was Fairyland! They saw a colourful palace and they wanted to go in.
Happily they ran along the glittery path.
Suddenly they saw a pretty, sad fairy.
'My name is Sparkly.'
She told them a smelly ogre was taking sweets.
Ben and Emma found the stinky ogre. They told him the fairy was sad.
He said, 'Find my yummy house and then I will give back the sweets.'
On the way they met a talking pony who told them the way. Soon they found the yummy house.
They had a party. There was cake, balloons and presents.
Eventually it was time to go. Their new friends gave Ben and
Emma beautiful presents. Finally they opened the magic door.

Mia Jenks (5)
Lawley Primary School, Lawley

Lexie's Jungle Story

... a dark, scary jungle.

They began to swing on the green vines and they felt happy.

'This is fun!' shouted Ben and Emma.

All of a sudden, they bumped into an angry, sly snake. The sly snake hissed. 'I'm going to eat you!' Scared for their lives, they started to run. However the hungry snake didn't give up. He was getting closer and closer.

Fortunately they met a friendly lion. He said, 'Hello, how can I help you?'

The children cried, 'There is an angry snake chasing after us. Can you help us get back home?' The lion said, 'Climb on my furry back.'

The children were delighted to be back at the magic door.

Lexie Hendrie (6)
Lawley Primary School, Lawley

Noah's Magical Story

... an amazing land. It was Sweety Land. They saw a sweety palace and they wanted to go in.

Happily they ran along the rainbow path.

Suddenly they saw a pretty, sad fairy.

'My name is Glitter.' She told them a smelly ogre was stopping parties.

Ben and Emma found the stinky ogre. They told him the fairy was sad.

He said, 'Find my Haribo house and I will give back the sweets.'

On the way a talking dog told them the way. Soon they found the yummy house and the spell was broken!

The new friends had a party. There was music, jelly and party hats.

Eventually it was time to go. Their friends gave Ben and Emma rainbow presents. Finally they opened the magic door.

Noah Dungey (6)
Lawley Primary School, Lawley

Jake's Space Story

... space! Emma and Ben saw shiny stars and they were surrounded with black space! They had to wear spacesuits and helmets. They were floating in space.

They landed on Planet Gongons and started to pick stars. Behind them was an alien, he was green. He was a cute little alien.

Suddenly, a big spaceship saw them! It had green and yellow lights flashing Emma and Ben were scared. The dog barked.

The alien needed friends to play with. He was a very friendly alien. They had a very bumpy ride on the spaceship.

All of a sudden, a huge monster tried to eat them up in one gulp! They squashed him!

Emma and Ben said, 'See you another time.'

The alien said, 'Bee Blob.'

Jake Sheen (5)
Lawley Primary School, Lawley

Sebastien's Magical Story

... an amazing land! It was Sweetie Land! There was a shiny, gold path! Happily they ran along the rainbow path.

Suddenly, they saw a pretty, sad fairy.

'My name is Poppy!' She told them a smelly ogre was stealing all the sweeties.

Ben and Emma found the ogre. They told him the fairy was sad.

He said, 'Find my chocolate house and I will give back the sweeties.'

On the way they met a talking rabbit who told them the way. Soon they found the delicious house and the spell was broken!

The new friends had a party. There were hot doughnuts and cakes and ice cream.

Eventually it was time to go home. Their friends gave presents to Ben and Emma. Finally they opened the magic door.

Sebastien Troy Smith (6)

Lawley Primary School, Lawley

Niall's Jungle Story

... a dark, scary jungle. They began to swing on vines and they felt happy.

'This is fun!' shouted Ben.

All of a sudden, they bumped into an angry sly snake. The snake hissed, 'I'm going to eat you!' They were scared to death. They tried to run. However the snake didn't give up, he was getting closer and closer.

Fortunately they met a friendly lion. He said, 'Hello, how can I help you?'

The children cried, 'There's a snake after us. Can we go on your back to the magic door?'

'Yes, why is there a snake after you?'

'We don't know.'

When were back at the magic door, they went back home.

Niall Corrigan (6)
Lawley Primary School, Lawley

Oscar's Jungle Story

... a dark scary jungle. They began to swing on the green vines and they felt happy.

'This is fun! shouted Ben.

All of a sudden, they bumped into an angry, slimy snake, it hissed, 'I'm going to eat you!'

Scared for their lives, they started to run.

However the hungry snake didn't give up. He was getting closer and closer!

Fortunately they met a friendly lion. He said, 'Hello, how can I help you?'

The children cried, 'There is a creepy snake chasing us!' Can you help us get back home?'

The friendly lion replied, 'Climb onto my back.' The children were delighted to find themselves back at the magic door.

Oscar Chamera (6)
Lawley Primary School, Lawley

Isaac's Jungle Story

... a dark, scary jungle. They began to swing on the vines and they felt happy.

'This is fun!' shouted Ben.

All of a sudden, they bumped into an angry, sly snake! The snake hissed, 'I'm going to eat you!' Scared for their lives, they started to run.

However the hungry snake didn't give up. He was getting closer and closer!

Fortunately they met a friendly lion. He said, 'Hello, how can I help you?'

The children cried, 'There is an angry snake after us, can you help us get back home?'

The lion kindly replied, 'Climb onto my furry back.' The children were delighted to find themselves back at the magic door.

Isaac Oliver Darbyshire (5)

Lawley Primary School, Lawley

Jack's Jungle Story

... a dark, scary jungle. They began to swing on the vines and they felt happy. 'This is fun!' shouted Emma and Ben and the dog.

All of a sudden, they bumped into an angry snake! The snake hissed, 'I'm going to eat you all up!' Scared to death, they started to run. However the angry snake didn't give up! He was getting closer and closer.

Fortunately they met a friendly lion. He said, 'Hello, how can I help you?'

The children cried, 'There's an angry snake chasing us. Can you help us get back home?'

The lion kindly replied, 'Climb onto my furry back.'

The children were delighted to find themselves back at the magic door.

Jack Oliver Jones (6)
Lawley Primary School, Lawley

Angel's Magical Story

... an amazing land. It was a Party Land. They saw a pink palace. Happily they ran along a blue path. Suddenly they saw a pretty, sad fairy.

'My name is Trinket.'

She told them a smelly ogre was stopping parties.

Ben and Emma found the stinky ogre, they told him the fairy was sad.

He said, 'Find my chocolate house and I will give you the sweets.'

On the way they met a talking cat who told them the way. Soon they found the tasty house.

The new friends had a party. There was music, jelly and food.

Eventually it was time to go. The new friends gave Ben and Emma big presents. Finally they opened the magic door.

Angel Antwi (5)

Lawley Primary School, Lawley

Lyra's Magical Story

... an amazing land. It was Sweets Land! They saw a sweetie castle and wanted to go
in. Happily they skipped along the glittery rainbow path.
Suddenly they saw a pretty, sad fairy.
'My name is Amy.' She told them a smelly ogre had stolen some fairy sweets.
Ben and Emma found the smelly ogre. They told the ogre that the fairy was sad.
He replied, 'Find my gold house and you will find the sweets!'
On the way they met a talking frog, he told them the way. Soon they were at the gold house and the spell was broken!
The new friends had a party, there were pancakes, balloons and music.
'Time to go home!' so they went home.

Lyra Jones (5)
Lawley Primary School, Lawley

Ray's Space Story

... space! Emma and Ben saw sparkly stars. Suddenly, they saw pitch-black, they felt terrified! Emma and Ben landed on Planet Poop. They were picking shiny gold and yellow stars but behind them was a cheeky blue alien.

Suddenly, the alien got his bleep blowing ship. Emma and Ben were worried. It sucked them up. The dog was barking.

The alien was nice. He just wanted to tell jokes. The ship was bumping very fast. They actually became friends.

Then a fat monster tried to get his tongue on the ship to steal the spaceship. And then their gas went out. They defeated him.

The alien dropped them off on Earth. He said, 'Bleep blop.'

Ray Joseph Malone (6)
Lawley Primary School, Lawley

Elle's Jungle Story

... a dark scary jungle. They began to swing on the vines and they felt happy.

'This is fun!' shouted Ben.

All of a sudden, they bumped into a snake. It hissed, 'I'm going to eat you!'

Scared to death, they started to run. However the hungry snake didn't give up, he was getting closer and closer.

Fortunately they met a friendly lion. He said, 'Hello! How can I help you?'

The children cried, 'There is a snake chasing us. How can we get home?'

The lion kindly replied. 'Climb on my furry back.'

The children were delighted to find they were home.

Elle Clifton (6)
Lawley Primary School, Lawley

Grace's Space Story

... space! Emma and Ben saw twinkling stars as they floated around the galaxy. They felt very surprised!

Meanwhile, they landed on Mars. They wanted to pick stars. They were introduced to a cheeky pink alien who wanted to suck them up!

Suddenly, they were sucked up by the blue and green spaceship. Emma didn't like blue. Ben didn't like green.

Fortunately the alien was lovely, he decided to take them for a ride.

'Oh no!' shouted Ben. 'Look, a monster, quick shine a light on him!' As quick as a flash the monster disappeared, never to be seen again.

'Goodbye,' said the alien.

Grace Simpson (6)

Lawley Primary School, Lawley

Emma's Magical Story

... an amazing land. Sweets Land. They saw a pink palace and wanted to go in. Happily they walked on.

Suddenly they saw a pretty, sad fairy.

'My name is Annabelle.'

She told them a smelly ogre was stealing all the sweets.

Ben and Emma found the stinky ogre. They told him the fairy was sad.

He said, 'Find my chocolate house and I will give back the sweets.'

On the way they met a talking toad who told them the way. Soon they found the tasty house. The spell was broken.

They had a party with their friends. They ate hot dogs.

It was time to go. Their new friends gave Ben and Emma nice presents.

Emma Alice Wagg (5)
Lawley Primary School, Lawley

Darcy's Space Story

... space. Emma and Ben were in pitch-black and they were picking stars. They were happy and the dog was too.

Emma and Ben landed on a planet, Sweet Land. They started picking the glowing stars. There was a bright pink alien. It was a sad alien.

Suddenly a spaceship appeared, it was rainbow coloured. Emma and Ben were screaming, 'Help!'

Emma and Ben were friends with the alien. He was shy and nice. They were nice to each other for now.

A slimy, big monster was trying to eat them.

They zapped him and he ran away.

'Goodbye!' Emma and Ben said.

'You too!' said the alien.

Darcy Glaze (6)
Lawley Primary School, Lawley

Joshua's Magical Story

... an amazing land. It was Party Land! They saw a sparkly palace. They wanted to go in. Happily they ran along the glittery path.
Suddenly they saw a pretty, sad fairy.
'My name is Poppy.'
She told them a smelly ogre was stealing sweets.
Ben and Emma found the stinky ogre. They told him the fairy was sad.
He said, 'Find my house and I will give back the sweets.'
On the way they met a frog who told them the way.
They found the tasty house and the spell broke!
The new friends had a party. There was music, a table of food and party hats.
Eventually it was time to go.

Joshua Williams (6)
Lawley Primary School, Lawley

Daisy's Superhero Story

... Money Land! They saw shiny flowers and small statues. They felt lonely.

Suddenly a robber came, picked the flowers and put them in the sack. Emma and Ben were disappointed.

They found the robber and had a magnificent argument. Emma and Ben were feeling brave, so they called the police.

The robber was put in jail so he was feeling angry Emma and Ben and the dog got a card for saving the day. They wanted to share the cards but there weren't enough.

They flew home with their cards and had a pyjama party.

Daisy Iris Dawes (6)

Lawley Primary School, Lawley

Euan's Space Story

... space! Emma and Ben were floating and they saw glistening stars and it was black all around them!

Emma and Ben landed on Planet Zig and Zog and they were picking stars. Behind them was a blue alien!

Suddenly, the blue alien sucked Emma and Ben and the dog into his flying saucer. The dog was barking!

They had a ride in the flying saucer! He went very fast and bumpy!

Then they saw an ugly huge monster and they used the laser beam on his eyeball and then he ran off!

Emma and Ben got dropped off and said, 'Bobo bee eu doooo oooo ooo oooooo!'

Euan O'Neil (6)
Lawley Primary School, Lawley

Jack's Magical Story

... a beautiful castle. It was so shiny they wanted to go in.

But on their way they saw a talking worm and it told them where to go.

'Just follow the path please.'

When they got to the castle they saw a stinky and green ogre and the ogre said, 'Follow me.' And he took them to his house and it was made out of Haribos and they went inside.

The children said, 'Shall we have a party?'

'Yes!' the ogre said, they brought cake, presents and party hats.

Finally they were delivering presents to everyone.

Jack Robert Hughes (5)

Lawley Primary School, Lawley

Lilia's Space Story

... space! Emma and Ben saw shiny stars. They were wearing space helmets and they felt happy and jolly!

Emma and Ben landed on Planet Joopy. They were picking stars for their mum and dad. Behind them there was a camouflaged alien.

Suddenly, a beeping spaceship appeared. The dog started to worry and they were scared.

The friendly alien was zooming and playing Tig and Simon Says with Emma and Ben.

Then a weird alien tried to eat them. They tried to shoot laser beams.

They were back on Earth, the alien said goodbye.

Lilia Green (6)
Lawley Primary School, Lawley

Peramvir's Superhero Story

... Dino Land! They saw baby dinosaurs relaxing. The dinosaurs were friendly. They were happy. Suddenly, a robber came and stole the happy dinosaur's egg. Emma and Ben were worried. They found the robber and he turned in the dinosaur's egg. They put the egg back secretly. Emma and Ben were happy.

The robber was in jail. He was annoyed.

Ben and Emma got medals and they were happy. Emma and Ben flew home. They were tired so they went to bed.

Peramvir Chaudhari (6)

Lawley Primary School, Lawley

Jacoby's Space Story

... space. Emma and Ben saw glittery stars. They both felt happy.
Emma and Ben landed on the moon,
they started picking stars. Behind them was an alien.
Suddenly a beeping, flashing spaceship appeared. Emma and Ben were sucked up into the spaceship. They were scared.
The alien was friends with them. They zoomed fast through space.
A big, horrible monster appeared right behind them! They squashed them.
They landed back on Earth.

Jacoby Perry (6)
Lawley Primary School, Lawley

Charlotte's Superhero Story

... Pugland. Little pugs ran around everywhere. The sun shone. They were joyful!

Suddenly, the robber came and took Ben! He put Ben in the sack. The robber ran. Ben was bad and he was sleepy. He fell asleep.

Emma called the police.

The robber got in trouble. The robber got taken to jail. 'Aw!' said the robber.

Emma and Ben got a trophy!

'Wow!' said Emma. 'It's pretty!'

They flew home and went to school to tell their friends.

Charlotte Williams (6)

Lawley Primary School, Lawley

Manahal's Superhero Story

... Superhero Land! They saw
flying superheroes. The superheroes had
colourful clothes! They were happy.
Suddenly, a robber came and stole a big butterfly.
Emma and Ben were angry!
They saw the robber and the other superheroes
came to help. They had a fight and the robber got
punched! They called the police.
The robber was in jail and felt annoyed.
Emma and Ben got a sticker and a medal. They
were excited.
They flew home and played superheroes.

Manahal Maqbool (6)
Lawley Primary School, Lawley

Logan's Superhero Story

It took them to Star Wars Land! They saw lots of bright lightsabers! They saw Kylo Ren and they felt scared.

Suddenly, a robber came and stole all of the gold lightsabers. Emma and Ben were scared.

They saw the robber and they had a fight! Ben and Emma felt brave.

The robber went to jail and felt sad.

Emma and Ben got a sword from Kylo Ren! They were shocked!

Emma and Ben watched Star Wars on TV and played with their new swords. They had a good play.

Logan Round (6)

Lawley Primary School, Lawley

Maddie's Superhero Story

... Superhero Land! They saw flying superheroes with colourful capes. They felt happy. Suddenly, a robber came and took the superheroes. Emma and Ben were sad.

They saw the robber and had a humongous argument. The robber was scared and they called the cops.

The robber was in jail but he was sneaky. He tried to escape!

Emma and Ben felt sad because they put someone in jail, but he had been naughty.

They went home and watched TV.

Maddie French (6)

Lawley Primary School, Lawley

Ava's Superhero Story

... Tay Land. They could see Spidergirl and a colourful rainbow. They were happy and joyful!
Then a robber came and stole Spidergirl! Emma and Ben were sad and alone.
The dog was scared. Emma and Ben were brave and the robber was really scared! They then called the Police!
The robber went into jail and was scared!
Emma and Ben got a rosette and Emma got a medal.
Emma and Ben flew home and played superheroes all day and night.

Ava McGlynn (6)
Lawley Primary School, Lawley

Lexi's Space Story

... space. Emma and Ben saw shiny stars, they were happy and excited!

Emma and Ben landed on Planet Socks.

They started picking stars. Behind them was an alien with red eyes.

Suddenly, a red and blue spaceship appeared. Emma and Ben were sucked up! They were scared.

The alien was kind. It was fast.

A mean and horrible monster tried eating them.

The spaceship squashed him.

They landed back on Earth.

Lexi Watson (5)
Lawley Primary School, Lawley

Erin's Superhero Story

... Butterfly Land! They saw fluffy and colourful butterflies! They felt joyful.

Suddenly, a robber came and stole all of the butterflies! Emma and Ben were scared.

Emma and Ben called the police and the robber was scared.

The robber went to jail and was never allowed out again! The robber was scared.

Emma and Ben got an award and they were excited!

Emma and Ben flew back home and had a butterfly party and they were all happy!

Erin Rogers (5)
Lawley Primary School, Lawley

Mikael's Superhero Story

... Lego Land! They saw wild cats all around them. They felt excited!

Suddenly, a robber came and stole some money. Emma and Ben were angry.

Emma and Ben saw the robber and had a fight, but they did a karate kick and he went to jail and he couldn't get out.

The robber was in jail for two million years and was sad.

Emma and Ben got medals and they were happy! They flew home and told their mum and dad.

Mikael Hasnain (6)

Lawley Primary School, Lawley

William's Superhero Story

... Florida! They saw some rabbits jumping in the sunshine!

The robber came and he stole the rabbits. Emma and Ben were so disappointed!

The robber was scared and gave the rabbits back. Emma and Ben were scared, so they called the police.

The robber was put in jail. He was angry!

Emma and Ben spoke to him and set him free.

They flew home and played heroes.

William Augustus Bear Jones (5)

Lawley Primary School, Lawley

Millie's Superhero Story

... Candy Land! They saw a dog running and lots of candy. They felt happy.

Suddenly, a robber came and stole all of the candy. Emma and Ben were mad.

They saw the robber and they called the police! Emma and Ben were happy,

the robber went to jail and felt so sorry.

Emma and Ben got a well-done badge They were so happy!

Emma and Ben flew home and played in the garden.

Millie Bracken (6)
Lawley Primary School, Lawley

Lilliana's Superhero Story

... Lego Land! They could see wild cats miaowing. They felt nervous.

Suddenly, a robber came and stole all of the cats. Emma and Ben were frightened!

They saw the robber and had a fight. They got the bag and got the cats out.

The robber was put in a jail and he was frightened.

Emma and Ben got a gun. They were surprised!

They flew home and played superheroes.

Lilliana Jean Corsentino (6)

Lawley Primary School, Lawley

Eva's Superhero Story

... Superhero Land! They had colourful hair and scary capes. They were happy.
Suddenly, a robber came and stole lots of superheroes. Emma and Ben were upset!
The superheroes escaped from the robber. They had a big fight.
The robber got put in jail. He was annoyed.
Emma and Ben got a sticker, they were happy.
They flew home to celebrate!

Eva Kaur Sandhu (6)
Lawley Primary School, Lawley

Poppy's Jungle Story

... a tropical jungle. Then from the door there were three vines. One for Emma, one for Ben and one for the dog. They swung on the vines with excitement, not knowing that one of the vines was actually a vine snake! They immediately let go of the snake. The snake said in a hollow voice, 'I can show you the way to the magic door. Follow me.' Emma, Ben and dog followed. But suddenly the snake led them into a trap! The snake started to spit poison.

'Aaah!' they said. They ran through the jungle and lost the snake. The dog started barking at an orange bush that turned out to be a lion.

Emma was worried and asked, 'Wh-who are you?'

'My name is Sam,' said the lion.

Sam bent down and Emma, Ben and dog got on Sam cautiously.

'Where are you taking us?' asked Ben.

'To the magic door!' said Sam.

'Look, there is the door!' said Emma.

So Sam said, 'Bye-bye!' and Emma, Ben and dog climbed up three green vines and swung, vine by vine, down to the magic door.

Poppy Ann Hannah (6)

Wymondley JMI School, Little Wymondley

Heer's Jungle Story

... a scary jungle. They saw some green vines, they swung on them, but one was a scary snake. They let go and fell on the leafy ground. The snake said, 'Hello,' in a low voice.

Emma whispered to Ben, 'Let's get out of here.'

The snake said, 'Where are you going?'

'Home.'

'Why don't you want to stay here?'

'You're going to eat us!'

'Run, Ben and dog! As fast as you can, the snake is chasing us!'

'Yes you're right! Go, go go! come on dog! Faster, faster dog! Faster! Be careful dog, don't let him eat you.'

Then they saw a lion, they thought it was a scary one, but it's a nice lion.

'Are you nice lion?'

'Yes, I am, why?'

'We are lost, can you give us a ride?'

'Yes sure. Hop on!' And then they did.

'Go faster! Wee! Wee! This is so much fun!'

'It is!'

'Hold on tight, here we go!'

'Faster and faster, this is fun!'
'Very fun you mean!'
'There's the magic door, let's get to it!'
'Quick before it moves, quick, quick we are nearly there.'
'Let's run very fast so we can get through the door.'

Heer Trushar Thakkar (5)
Wymondley JMI School, Little Wymondley

Alice's Jungle Story

... a jungle. They found a big lumpy rock and when they jumped off, to their surprise, they got tangled up in the long vines. Emma, Ben and the dog started swinging on the vines. They were having such good fun, that they didn't realise that one of the vines was a green, slimy snake.
They screamed and let go of the snake and they fell onto a soft branch.
'Hello,' said the snake, in a sly voice.
Ben whispered to Emma, 'We better get out because he looks like he might want to eat us.' Ben was right. The snake went to eat them up.
Emma, Ben and the dog ran as fast as they could, away from the snake. At last they lost the snake.
After losing the snake they met a friendly lion. The lion said, 'Hello my name is George.'
They asked the lion if he could help them. Emma said, 'We are lost because we got chased by a ferocious snake. And we need to get back to the magical door.'
The lion said, 'OK I will help you.' So the lion bent down very carefully and Emma, Ben and the dog climbed on the lion's back nervously. The lion ran at top speed through the jungle, to the magical door in the tree.

They went through the door and it took them back home where they had some delicious dinner.

Alice Philippa Bestford (6)

Wymondley JMI School, Little Wymondley

Jessica's Magical Story

... Sweety Fairy Land. On the other side of the door everything was made from chocolate and sweets. 'Wow! Look at that door, it's made from chocolate and the handle's made from a sweet!' said Ben. 'Hi,' said a voice on a tasty mushroom. 'Woof!' barked the dog. 'Wow!' said Emma and Ben. 'I'm Jenny, welcome to Sweety Fairy Land!' 'It smells like candy,' said Emma. Then Emma said to Ben, 'What a stinky smell.' 'I think it smells like fluff and dustbins,' said Ben. 'Yuck!' said Emma. 'Hi,' said the monster. 'Sorry about the smell.' 'That's OK,' said Emma. 'We rather worry about your house. Our dog is eating it!' 'Never mind,' said the goblin. 'Let's throw a party!' said the goblin, 'And Jenny can come too.' 'A fun, super party you mean?' said Ben. 'Let's party!' said Jenny. When they got home they still had their presents.

Jessica Stappard (5)
Wymondley JMI School, Little Wymondley

Daisy's Jungle Story

... the Amazon jungle! Emma was so excited. She felt the sun roasting her skin. Then Ben saw a vine and started to climb. It was very long and green. When they found an exit, Ben showed Emma and the dog a picture of what they were looking for. It was the blue poisonous parrot! They were very excited. Then they set off.

One day later, Emma, Ben and the dog walked around exploring the Amazon.

Then Emma shouted, 'Guys, guys! I saw the parrot!'

They chased it and chased it until they came across a lion! It roared loudly. But they weren't scared, so they moved on.

They finally caught up with it and as it settled down on a branch, they caught it in the cage! They identified it and it was going to have baby parrots.

So they let it go and went back to the secret door for supper.

Daisy Elizabeth Fraser (7)

Wymondley JMI School, Little Wymondley

131

Freddie's Magical Story

... Sweetie Land. And they saw that the door was made of chocolate and caramel.

'Mmm!' said Ben.

'Wow!' said Emma.

They saw a gingerbread house and it has gummy bears. The dog barked.

Emma said, 'Maybe he wants to go in the house.' So they opened the chocolate door but it started to melt!

'Oh no!' Chocolate was melting on Ben.

'Argh! Help!'

Emma had an idea, she got the frisbee and tried to throw it by the door. *Crash! Bang! Wallop!* The door broke.

'Ouch!' Ben was OK inside. Then there was a cake and it had two candles. They found a knife and cut it in half and ate the cake.

'Mmm, delicious! Now let's go through the magic door. So what are we waiting for?'

Freddie Moore (6)

Wymondley JMI School, Little Wymondley

Isaac's Jungle Story

... the jungle. When they walked through the jungle, they went on the vines but suddenly they screamed because one of the vines was a vine snake! Emma and Ben didn't know.

The snake said, 'Hello, my name is Erik.' Erik was frustrated.

Ben said, 'Let's get out of here!'

They sprinted and suddenly they lost Erik the snake.

Suddenly, they met a friendly lion. 'Hello my name is Alice!'

'Woof,' said the dog.

'Hello, I'm Emma.'

'And I'm Ben.'

Alice asked, 'Do you want to ride on my back?'

Everyone said, 'Yes. please!'

Emma and Ben and the dog got on Alice's back.

They swung on the vines and sang.

'Awuhaayaawuyay!'

They said goodbye to Alice.

Isaac Page (6)

Wymondley JMI School, Little Wymondley

William's Magical Story

... a gingerbread house. Emma and Ben walked through the door and through the gingerbread house. They came out of the gingerbread house. Emma and Ben saw a chocolate fairy sitting on a sweetie mushroom.

Emma and Ben saw a chocolate goblin and Emma and Ben walked away because the goblin was smelly.

Emma and Ben followed the goblin to a gingerbread man's house.

Emma and Ben had a party at the goblin's house and Emma and Ben had so much fun, and the dog was jumping and running around.

Emma and Ben had cake and it was so delicious and Emma and Ben had more cake.

William Watts (6)
Wymondley JMI School, Little Wymondley

Alfie's Space Story

... space. They fell into a flying saucer and they saw an alien. The alien mind-read Emma and Ben. They were thinking whatever the alien said. The alien was dotty and it had 1000 eyes.
The alien took them home.

Alfie Robin Handley (8)

Wymondley JMI School, Little Wymondley

The Storyboards

Here are the fun storyboards children could choose from...

Jungle

Magical

Pirate

Space

Superhero

First published in Great Britain in 2018 by:

Young Writers
Remus House
Coltsfoot Drive
Peterborough
PE2 9BF
Telephone: 01733 890066
Website: www.youngwriters.co.uk

Young Writers
Information

We hope you have enjoyed reading this book and
that you will continue to in the coming years.

If you're a young writer who enjoys reading and creative
writing, or the parent of an enthusiastic poet or story writer,
do visit our website **www.youngwriters.co.uk**. Here you
will find free competitions, workshops and games, as well
as recommended reads, a poetry glossary and our blog.

If you would like to order further copies of this book, or any of
our other titles give us a call or visit **www.youngwriters.co.uk**.

Young Writers
Remus House
Coltsfoot Drive
Peterborough
PE2 9BF

(01733) 890066
info@youngwriters.co.uk